JUNIOR
GRAPHIC NOVEL

D0097054

DISNEY'S Lilo & Stitch

Adapted by Greg Ehrbar

Artwork by Massimiliano Narciso
Anna Merli
Sonia Matrone
Gabriella Matta
Federico Bertolucci
Dario Calabria

DISNEY
PRESS

New York

Copyright © 2006 Disney Enterprises, Inc.

The name, image and likeness of Elvis Presley are used courtesy of Elvis Presley Enterprises, Inc.
No part of this book may be reproduced or transmitted in any form or by any means, electronic or mechanical, including photocopying, recording, or by any information storage and retrieval system, without written permission from the publisher. For information address Disney Press, 114 Fifth Avenue, New York, New York 10011-5690.

Printed in the United States of America
First U.S. Edition
1 3 5 7 9 10 8 6 4 2
Library of Congress Catalog Card Number: 2005910972
ISBN 1-4231-0141-3

HE IS BULLETPROOF, FIREPROOF, AND CAN THINK *FASTER* THAN A SUPERCOMPUTER. HE CAN SEE IN THE DARK AND MOVE OBJECTS *THREE THOUSAND* TIMES HIS SIZE. HIS ONLY MISSION...TO DESTROY EVERYTHING HE TOUCHES! HA-HA-HA-HA-HA-HA!

IT IS NOT *NATURAL!* IT MUST BE *DESTROYED!*

CALM YOURSELF, CAPTAIN GANTU. PERHAPS IT CAN BE *REASONED* WITH.

EXPERIMENT 626, GIVE US SOME SIGN YOU UNDERSTAND ANY OF THIS. SHOW US THERE IS SOMETHING INSIDE YOU THAT IS *GOOD.*

MEEGA NA LA *QUEESTA!*

SO NAUGHTY!

I DIDN'T TEACH HIM *THAT!*

PLACE THAT EVIL SCIENTIST UNDER *ARREST!*

AS FOR THAT *ABOMINATION*, IT IS THE FLAWED PRODUCT OF A DERANGED MIND. IT HAS NO PLACE AMONG US. CAPTAIN GANTU, TAKE HIM AWAY!

I PREFER TO BE CALLED EVIL *GENIUS!* HA-HA!

LATER, IN THE PRISON OF THE FEDERATION TRANSPORT SHIP *DURGON...*

UNCOMFORTABLE? *GOOD.* THE COUNCIL HAS BANISHED YOU TO EXILE ON A DISTANT ASTEROID...

...AND THESE GUNS ARE LOCKED ONTO YOUR GENETIC SIGNATURE. THEY ONLY SHOOT *YOU.*

OWW! WHY YOU LITTLE...!

5

WE HAVE TO GAS THE PLANET.

HOLD IT! EARTH IS A *PROTECTED WILDLIFE RESERVE.* WE'VE BEEN USING IT TO REBUILD THE ENDANGERED *MOSQUITO* POPULATION.

WE CAN'T, MR....?

PLEAKLEY. AND NO! THE MOSQUITOES' FOOD OF CHOICE, *HUMANOIDS,* LIVE THERE.

WHAT IF OUR MILITARY FORCES JUST *LANDED* THERE?

THAT WOULD BE A BAD IDEA. THESE ARE EXTREMELY *SIMPLE* CREATURES. LANDING THERE WOULD CREATE PLANETWIDE *PANIC.*

WHO THEN, *MR.* PLEAKLEY, WOULD *YOU* SEND FOR THE EXTRACTION?

DOES THE EXPERIMENT HAVE A BROTHER...?

A FEW MOMENTS LATER, AT THE MAXIMUM SECURITY PRISON...

...MAYBE A FRIENDLY COUSIN?

...OR A NEIGHBOR WITH A *BEARD?*

IN A PRISON CELL SITS A FRUSTRATED JUMBA...

AARGH!

EEEEEYAAAGHH!

626 GOT AWAY?

YES. AND NOW *YOU* MUST BRING HIM BACK, IN EXCHANGE FOR YOUR FREEDOM.

B-BUT WHO'S GOING TO *CONTROL* JUMBA?

7

9

WHEN LILO'S SISTER NANI REACHES THE HULA SCHOOL...

LILO? *LILO?* OH, NO.

YOU BETTER BE HOME!

WATCH WHERE YOU'RE GOING! *STUPID HEAD!*

SCREEEGH!

LILO? OPEN THE DOOR, LILO!

GO AWAY.

I'M NOT TALKING TO YOU!

YOU HAVE THREE DAYS TO CHANGE MY MIND AND PROVE YOU ARE RESPONSIBLE ENOUGH TO TAKE CARE OF LILO.

LILO, WHY DIDN'T YOU WAIT AT THE SCHOOL? DO YOU WANT TO BE TAKEN AWAY? YOU ARE *SUCH* A PAIN.

SO WHY DON'T YOU SELL ME AND BUY A *RABBIT*? THEN YOU'LL BE HAPPY, BECAUSE IT WILL BE *SMARTER* THAN ME!

AND QUIETER!

YOU'LL LIKE IT BECAUSE IT'S STINKY LIKE YOU!

GO TO YOUR ROOM!

SLAM!

I'M ALREADY IN MY ROOM!

AAAAAAAAAA!!!! AAAAAAAAAAA!!!!

LATER, NANI AND LILO HAVE CALMED DOWN...

I BROUGHT YOU SOME PIZZA.

ARE WE A BROKEN FAMILY?

A LITTLE... BUT I SHOULDN'T YELL AT YOU.

I LIKE YOU BETTER AS A *SISTER* THAN A MOM.

16

18

GRRRR...

WHEN YOU ARE READY TO *GIVE UP,* JUST LET US KNOW!

CATCHUCK-A! CATCHUCK-A!

HMMMM...

THIS IS YOU. THIS IS YOUR *BADNESS* LEVEL. IT'S UNUSUALLY HIGH FOR SOMEONE YOUR SIZE.

LILO, YOUR DOG CANNOT SIT AT THE TABLE.

STITCH IS TROUBLED. HE NEEDS *DESSERT.*

LOOK, *DAVID!* I GOT A NEW DOG!

WHOA! YOU *SURE* IT'S A DOG?

UH-HUH. HE USED TO BE A *COLLIE* BEFORE HE GOT RUN OVER.

YUM!

HEY!

YUCK!

HI, DAVID. DID YOU CATCH FIRE AGAIN?

NO, JUST THE STAGE. NANI, I WAS WONDERING... IF YOU'RE NOT DOING ANYTHING THIS—

DAVID, I TOLD YOU. I *CAN'T.*

I'VE GOT A LOT TO DEAL WITH RIGHT NOW.

DON'T WORRY, DAVID. SHE LIKES YOUR FANCY HAIR. I READ HER *DIARY.*

SHE THINKS IT'S *FANCY?*

SNIFF SNIFF

29

LILO! LILO!

YOU *RUINED* EVERYTHING!

YOU'RE AN ALIEN?

GET *OUT* OF HERE!

I THOUGHT YOU'D BE DIFFICULT TO CATCH.

WR-R-R

NO! *STOP!*

LILO!

RR-RR FOOM!

OKAY, TALK! WHERE'S LILO? *TALK! I KNOW* YOU CAN!

OKAY, LILO...

HAH! YOU'RE UNDER ARREST!

FOOM!

GALACTIC COMMAND? *EXPERIMENT 626* IS IN CUSTODY!

43

45

WOW!

SWOOOSSSH!

DAVID! CAN YOU GIVE US A RIDE?

SURE, BUT I'LL HAVE TO MAKE **TWO TRIPS.**

WE CAPTURED 626!

TAKE HIM TO MY SHIP.

NO! LEAVE HIM ALONE!

HOLD ON.

I THINK WE SHOULD GET GOING...

JUMBA! YOU'RE THE CAUSE OF ALL THIS! IF IT WASN'T FOR **EXPERIMENT 626,** NONE OF THIS—

STITCH.

DOES STITCH HAVE TO GO ON THE SHIP?

YES.

CAN STITCH SAY GOOD-BYE?

YES.